Dastaan-E-Jindagi

Flairs and Glairs

Publication House

"Dastaan-E-Jindagi"

ISBN No: " 978-93-90799-91-6"
1st Edition
Language – English and Hindi

Flairs and Glairs
Publication House
Regd. Under MSME Act.

Disclaimer

This is a work of fiction and solely represent the thoughts of the corresponding authors of the articles. Our editors have tried their best to edit the content of all the authors and check the plagiarism.

All the write-ups in this book are unique and are only published in this book.

In case any plagiarism or error is found, only the author is responsible alone, and not the publisher or the Compilers.

Cover Designing and Book Formatting

Shubham Shah and Ishani Agarwal

Co authors

Shubham Shah (Founder Flairs and Glairs)
Ishani Agrawal (Co-f Founder Flairs and Glairs)
Sakshi Barad (Compiler)

1. Kareena Verma
2. Barbie Rani Kataki
3. Archishman Satpathy
4. Rajesh Satpate
5. Shaily Saroj
6. Priyanka Tiwari
7. Sahina Ghugha
8. Shreya Gupta
9. Maung Ibrahim
10. Rashmi Yadav
11. Govind Joshi
12. Sukriti Chauhan
13. Anjali Samundre
14. Raza Sahil
15. Sushant Kumar
16. Neha Singhal
17. Mousumi Sen
18. Sadhwika Suma
19. Titiksha Singhal
20. Priyanshi Mittal
21. Manisha Sharma
22. Pramesh Kumar
23. Shariq Sheikh
24. Krishna Naresh Hire
25. Ashish Bharti
26. Jyoti Soni

27. Pragati Kumar Shrivastava
28. Deepika Kumari
29. Prachi Sharma
30. Saumya Bhatia
31. Jitesh Soni
32. Nibraz Shameem
33. Vidya Kala Agrawal
34. Varun Gupta
35. Sumana Saha
36. Divyanshu Pandey
37. Megha
38. Khushi
39. Ajay Kher
40. Kalamkaar
41. Rutvik Borade
42. Vijeyata Joshi
43. Rachiyata
44. Nasreena
45. Shubham Borade
46. Ann Goka
47. Safeer Bhola
48. Ann Goka
49. Saurabh Tripathi
50. Sarabjot Purba

Shubham Shah

(Founder- Flairs and Glairs)

Shubham Shah, an entrepreneur at "Flairs & Glairs" a brand with dynamics in events organizing and cultural educational pan INDIA, is a 26yrs old guy who recently has entered the digital platform of imprinting emotions. He has initiated with his own open mic platform to help budding poets and aspiring writers under his brand named as "Teekhe Zasbaaat"

He is a commerce graduate from the Bhagalpur City of Bihar. He states Writing has impersonated him since childhood and he has now been writing for over a decade!
Cooking, on the other hand, is his passion! He also mentions, trying out new things just tickles him!
When asked sir, Why SPICY EMOTIONS?
He smiled and added, "agar jasbaat teekhe na ho toh wo jasbaat kahan" Spices are all that blends! So do his words!
As a chef, he presents to you his dish! Hot and freshly served! Taste it! Feel it! Enjoy it! You can also find his writing in the Book "Teekhe Zasbaaat" and 50+ Co-authored anthologies. With his passion to explore opportunities across Platforms, he is working with keen devotion and We wish him all the very best for his future ventures.
He is Featured in the International Magazine DeMode for his upcoming solo novel.
He is Approved by Ne8x for its Lit Fest, and is a Golden Star Awards 2020 Winner.
He is a India Book of Records Holder for his Anthology Satrang, and has the Grandmaster title by Asia Book of Records, for the same.
He has also been featured in Prabhat Khabar, Dainik Jagran, and a lot of other Newspapers in Bihar for his achievements.
He has been a proud co-author to
India Book Of Records (Title- Black)
World Book Of Records (Title -15 Wonders of Poetries)
India Book Of Records (Title - Aaina)
Vajra World Records Holder (Title - Gustakhi Maaf Hai)
High Range of Records Holder (Title - Gustakhi Maaf Hai)
Indian Book of Records
(Title - Road from Worst to Best)

Share your reviews on his

INSTAGRAM

@spicy_emotions
@shubham4shah

Or via email on

shubham2shah@gmail.com

To stay tuned to his work and opportunities follow his business Handles

INSTAGRAM FACEBOOK YOUTUBE

@flairsandglairs
@teekhezasbaaat

WEBSITE:

https://flairsandglairs.in/
https://flairsandglairs.com/

Ishani Agarwal

(Co-Founder- Flairs and Glairs)

Ishani Agarwal hails from the City of Joy, Kolkata.

She is the co-founder of her Community "Teekhe Zasbaaat" and Flairs and Glairs Publication.

Been a Compiler for 45+ Anthologies, she is in the process for more. Co-authored in 150+ Anthologies. She is a India Book of Records Holder, a Vajra World Records Holder, a High Range of Records Holder, an OMG Book of Records Holder, a Bravo Record holder, a Forever Star Book of World Records and an Indian Book of Records Holder.

Approved by Ne8x for its Lit Fest 2020, and Literary Icon 2020. Also a Golden Star Awards Winner 2020.

She has also been awarded with India Star Republic Award 2021, a part of She Awards by Awards Arc and Winner of Nari Samman 2021 by Literoma.

She is also selected as Best Achiever of the Year by AwardsArc and Most Challenging Compiler Award by Spectrum Awards.
She got her first solo Published,a solo Compilation consisting of first 750 contents of hers, titled "Hand That Burnt While Healing".

She has been featured by the National Magazine "Taree Zameen Par" with the title 'unstoppable'.
Also featured in the International Magazine DeMode for her upcoming solo novel, she is proud to write on social issues, and is happy with the love she is receiving.
Connect with her on Instagram: @Ishani_agarwal_quotes / @compilations_so_far

Sakshi Barad

She is writer, orator, author and compiler from Nagpur, Maharashtra. She has completed her Postgraduation in Science. She is public speaker and Winner of many elocution and debate competitions, So awarded as Best Orator. She has represented her district in youth and student parliaments. She has also performed in poetry events.

She is published writer. She writes in Hindi, English and Marathi languages. She is passionate and hardworking and very good human being. Her interest and passion in art and literature inspires her to work in this field even if having a science background.

For contact – Instagram - @sakshibarad.5

Mail id – sakshibarad5@gmail.com

दास्तान ऐ जिंदगी

आमने सामने रहने वाले ऐसे भी कोई दोस्त थे,
सुबह से रात तक काम वो करतें थे..
रात को जब मिलते तोह खूब गप्पे लढाते..
दिन मे कीई सारी चिझे एक दुसरे को वो बताते..
एक दोस्त हमेशा अपनी अच्छी बाते बताता,
तो दुसरा रोज काही काम किया ऐसा कह कर मुह मुरझाता..
एक दोस्त सदा हसते रहता था,
लेकिन दूसरा अपनी जिंदगी बहुत दुखी था..
एक दिन उसने भगवानसे मन्नत माँगी,
"हे भगवान मेरे दोस्त को मिलनेवली सारी खुशियाँ तू मुझको दे दे "
भगवान ने उसकी सुन ली..
लेकिन दूसरे दिन से उसकी जिंदगी और भी दुखी हो गई..
वो भगवान को फिर बोला,
"क्यू तूने तेरे भक्त के साथ ऐसा खेल खेला ? "
भगवान ने उसे कहाँ ,"अरे मूर्ख तेरे दोस्त के पास से सुख तोह तब तुझे देता
जब उसके पास सचमे सुख होता"

तब उसे समझ आया था,
उसका दोस्त उससे भी बहुत दुखी था..
लेकिन फिर भी वह सदा मुस्कुराता रहता था..
दुनिया की रीत तो उसे समझ आ गई..
" यहाँ कोई रोकर दिल बहलाता है , तो कोई हँसकर दर्द छुपाता है "
दोस्त से उसे सुख तो नही मिला था..
लेकिन हँसना और जिंदगी जिने का तरीका जरूर मिल गया था...!!

एक दास्तान

कुछ बीते लम्हों को फ़िरसे दोहराये हम...
कुछ अनकही बातों को मुकाम तक ले जाए हम..
कुछ छुटी मुस्कुराहट को फ़िरसे सजाए हम..
क्या तेरा, क्या मेरा..छोड़..
सब मिलकर साथ निभाए हम..
चलो,
कुछ ऐसी एक दास्तान बनाए हम...
कुछ ऐसी एक दास्तान बनाए हम...!!

Kareena Verma

She is kareena verma The Daughter of Mr.Kehru verma & Mrs.Rajeshwari verma . She is a computer science student and currently pursuing the bachelor of application And she is very passionate in writing and co- author of many anthologies and as well as many international Anthologies too. In this world only her pen & diary is the best friend to penned her pain in the blank pages of life Diary .

And same as her name Kareena delineate alike her name , sanguine with her soul, pure with her heart , innocent with her straightforward thoughtful perceptions!

For her Rectitude within her is everything & nothing is above than Viracity with our nation , she wants only to flame alike terracotta Diya, for one day she'll spread the happiness of lights as the most bright star in the sky of someone home and just wanna to spread love of humanity every where !!

Dear Life

The life is full of find fault within me ,
Every time the pain inside me,
People won't let you live ,
People won't let you laugh,
But they're always be trying to see you
In terrible nights,
People won't let you live ,
But wanna see you in trauma!
But the sufferings pains inside you ,
Made you solide by heart !
The heart said to you ,
Be braveness within you !
Won't let you fall front of the stormy!
And the life has taught you,
The fearless girl inside you !

ऐ जिन्दगी.......

ऐ जिन्दगी,
तू हर पल साथ रहतीं हैं मेरे,
फिर क्यूं इतना तंग करतीं हैं मुझे।

तू कभी मुझे हारते हुए नहीं देख पाती,
इसलिए मुश्किलों से सामना करवा कर पाठ मुझे पढ़ाती।

तू यूंही साया बन रहना मेरा,
मेरे मां- बाबा सा ख़्याल रखना मेरा।

और हां! तुमसे कोई शिकवा नहीं है, बस थोड़ा सा कभी टूट सी जाती हु,
लेकिन तू मेरी सच्ची सखी बन हमेशा साथ निभाना मेरा।

हौसला बन हमेशा मेरा,
जिंदगी की हर नामुमकिन राहों में,
मुझे चलना सिखाना फ़र्ज़ है तेरा।

Barbie Rani Kataki

I write poems, short stories and I'm an occasional storyteller.

The Glance

The moment they shared a glance she could feel that something smashed inside her. At that one glance her heart recall memories of all the moments of their togetherness.Till then she used to think their separation was so traumatic and it'll take a lot of time to heal. Then after seeing him she thought why she took so much time to get this.This is life, people move on. May be we can't let go of someone easily no matter how badly we seperated because deep inside we still have hope. The hope of getting back, the hope of never getting replaced or forgotten.But now this glance made her realize everything. That he moved on, he became someone elses.

She jolted inside thinking about all those wakeful nights where it was too difficult for her to suddenly get used to his absence after years of being together. After some time she even stopped crying but that silence was killer. She has imagined almost every practical and impractical situations of his abrupt comebacks. But all the waits seems over now. Their separation was his selfish decision. She just followed him like always. May be that's where she was wrong.

But now it all seems fine. Not everything means to last a lifetime.Still right after the first encounter after five years she could think only one thing, that first glance of him in the library on her first day if college. She wished she could go back to that moment their glances met so that she would never turn back to the voice in the counter, "Hey listen are you Sukanya from newcomers?"

Archishman Satpathy

Archishman Satpathy, often called the Enthusiast Writer is a young dynamic writer from Deogarh, Odisha. He is presently pursuing B.Tech from IIIT Bhubaneswar. He started writing Quotes and Short Poetries from a young age of 16 and had now made it as his passion. He has contributed as co-author in more than 180 anthologies. He is the author of the book "LAKEEREIN ZINDAGI KE".

Perspective Of My Life

Even the way we thought of not having
It comes as like it is fed of describing
Like a unknown roadside wrangler
Taking the steps forward and striving
Having taught of the loss of happiness
Never tried unwanted except willingness
Just trying to complete the course assigned
The result be our perspective what defined
The past thorny path is now driving me
Towards a straightforward lucky victory
With self confidence from the heaven
For the honey to arrive and discover them
Making the path a little bit vast so strider
The turf of the hell need not be slide
For the health so healthy wealthy and wide
Luck always don't succeeded in chances
Passing the shrine for a blissful life
Dedication is today as sharp as the knife

Life In A Testimonial

Just trying to curse the luck now
And the life surprised me yet again
Never tried to thank dear life but
Quilling the ideas really very Sweven
Just thinking of the situation anyway
If those challenges won't be faced
Have I ever succeed in life without
A thick tricky armour of such shade
With the new moment I am enjoying
Testing the luck over hardwork today
And again life proved me complete wrong
This innocent and nuisance life is tricky
It may be as bad for some as a whiskey
But never harm anyone regardless their soul
Always teaches a person how to adore
Thank you life for such knowledge preaching
Hoping the holes are now happily filling

राजेश सतपते

राजेश सतपते उप्पूगुडा, शिवाजी नगर हैदराबाद का निवासी । वर्तमान में पीजीडीबीएम की पढ़ाई उस्मानिया विश्वविद्यालय से कर रहे है। एम.टेक, बीएससी, बी.टेक, किया है। परिवार में पापा और माताजी (श्री रामदास और श्रीमती कलवाती बाई सतपते का व्यवसाय चप्पल रिपेयरिंग का हैं) और छोटी प्यारी सी बहन हैं जिसका नाम सतपते सुनीता (बी ए - की पढ़ाई डॉ.बी आर अम्बेडकर सार्वत्रिक विश्विविद्यालय से की है। वर्तमान में एम बी ए की पढ़ाई करने जा रही हैं।) इन्होनें लेखन प्रतियोगिता 8 वर्ष की उम्र से किया है, बाल कविताएं, निबंध लेखन, कहानियां विद्यालय और विश्व विद्यलय में पढ़ते हुए " दैनिक हिन्दी मिलाप वार्ता पत्रिका" के माध्यम से की है। इन्हें अभी तक लेख , कहानी, व्यंग और कविता लेखन प्रतियोगिता में " दैनिक हिन्दी मिलाप वार्ता पत्रिका" की ओर से राष्ट्रीय स्तर पर पुरस्कार जानी मानी राज्य सरकार की राजनैतिक हस्तियों द्वारा प्रदान किया गया है।

संपर्क सूत्र : Instagram I'd : rajesh.Satpate
E-mail : smsrks18@gmail.com

ऐतबार

ऐ सनम मेरा एतबार हो तुम
मेरा जीवन हो, मेरा प्यार हो तुम।
ऐ सनम मेरा एतबार हो तुम।
पतझड़ के उजड़े गुलशन में,
फिर महकी है वह बाहर हो तुम
ऐ सनम मेरा एतबार हो तुम।
ऐ सनम मेरा एतबार हो तुम,
जिसने जीना मुझे सिखा दिया मुझको फिर मुझे से मिला दिया, मेरे जीवन का वह सार हो तुम।
ऐ सनम मेरा एतबार हो तुम,तेरे प्यार के की बारिश में भीगा मेरा सब तन मन आत्मा।
मुझे अंतर तक जो भीगा गया,उस अमृत की बौछार हो तुम।
ऐ सनम मेरा एतबार हो तुम,
मैं अंधेरी एक खाई थी, तुम दीपक बनकर आए हो।
मुझे को जगाने की खातिर, तुम दिलबर बनकर आए हो।
मेरे जीवन की खुशियों का, महका-महका सिंगार हो तुम।
ऐ सनम मेरा एतबार हो तुम मेरा जीवन हो मेरा प्यार हो तुम,,,,,

पाखंड

सच्च का रूप निराला,
सुख दुःख आता जाता।
पाखंडी भावना से,
ईश्वर हमें बचाता।।
पाखंड रचने वाला,
कुछ दिन ही चल पाता।
भेद सामने आता,
जीते जी मर जाता।।
पाखंड भरे जाल में,
अच्छे-अच्छे फस जाते।
जीवन में ये अवसर,
कई बार जो आते।।
पाखंडी इस चक्कर में,
नांव सबकी डूबी है।
नये शिकार ढूंढना,
इनकी यह खूबी है।।

Shaily Saroj

She is Shaily Saroj from Sangam nagri Prayagraj..
She is the student of Allahabad University..
Her hobbies are poetry writing singing and reading novels...

एक छोटी सी मुलाकात ज़िन्दगी से

कल मिली थी जिंदगी,
और पूछने लगी यार तुम थकती नहीं हो...
अच्छा चलो ये तो बता दो "कब है इरादा बिखरने का",
मैंने हंसकर कहा बिखर तो हम उस दिन ही गए थे,
जब पहली बार खाया था धोखा अपनों से,
जिंदगी ने सोचा पूछो कुछ और सवालात,
फिर मैंने ही रोका उसे,
और कहा बिखरी थीं बेशक पर अब समेट लिया है खुद को,
माना कि कुछ दरारे आ गई हैं,
पर इन दरारों में भी अब हमने उम्मीदें भर दी है।।।

ज़िन्दगी

ज़िन्दगी तेरा भी क्या कहना,
जीने की वजह भी छीन लेती हैं,
और मरने का रास्ता भी मोड़ लेती हैं,
अपनों को भी दूर करती है,
और अपनापन भी दिखाती हैं,
हर मोड़ पर मुश्किलें भी ला कर खड़ी करती,
और खुद ही उसे सुलझाने भी आ जाती है,
कोशिश बहुत करती हूं तुझे समझने की,
पर हर बार मै तुझमें और उलझ जाती है,
कभी तू मुझे आ कर बता तो सही,
आखिर तेरी रजा क्या है।।

Priyanka K. Tiwari

Priyanka had a poetic disposition from childhood on. Her first poem was published in a newspaper when she was 8. She has written many poems in English and Hindi, some of which appeared in local newspapers and magazines. A graduate in Biotechnology, she is currently associated with the field of HR- Organizational Psychology. Travelling, photography and reading are her passions. She can be reached at -

Instagram: @pri_at_insta
and via email at
words.verses.dreams@gmail.com

Nostalgia
(Best Days Of Life)

There are tears rolling from my eyes...
Tears of mourning- they do not tell lies!

I remember... the days I spent, as a child, with my friends,
Oh! how with age, mind gets corrupted and innocence ends!

In my memories, the childhood recollections,
Of those glorious days, are the reflections.

Had we not chased the squirrels, playing in the lanes?
And relished honey, mangoes, plums and sugarcanes?

Major chunk of our time spent in the playground,
Making sand castles or simply goofing around.

Oh! How we would just shout, yell and run!
Those frisky days, weren't they fun?

What a joy it was, to bunk the school!
And around the neighbourhood, to play the fool!

So oblivious were we, to time and clime!
So ignorant were we, of piety or crime!

True, my heart still pines away...
For the sand, where, as a child, I lay!

Today, life has given me so much to relish,
But those distant memories, I will forever cherish....!!!

Sahina Ghugha

Sahina Ghugha is 20 year old b.com student at Saurashtra university Rajkot. She is from Jamnagar city of Gujarat. She is state level winner in poetry competition 2017. She is Co-author of 10+ anthologies. She is an amazing writer and poet and she wants do something for society through her pen.
Insta ID:-
Itz_Sahina_write

ज़िन्दगी - एक पहेली

कभी हसाती है जी भर के
कभी रोने पे मजबूर करती हैं
कभी भावनाओं से पिगला देती
कभी पत्थर सा मजबूत कर देती है
कभी सपने टूटने का गम है
कभी अपनो के रूठने का गम
कभी शोर खामोशियों का है
कभी चुप्पी है अकेलेपन की
कभी बेवफाई पे रोती आंखे
कभी किसीको देख मुस्काते होठ
कभी मिलने की प्रार्थनाएं होती
कभी बिछड़ चुका वो जूठ
ज़िन्दगी की कश्मकश बड़ी भारी
सरदर्द सी ये एक पहेली है
फिर भी जीना पड़ेगा जीवन को
यही तो हमारी आखिर सहेली है।

Shreya Gupta

Writing is her passion. A strong believer in the power of positive thinking. Wants to serve the nation by fulfilling her future dream and ambition.
She is fond of dancing. Carries hope to kearn off all the time. Blend of sensible and sometimes a funny form.

"हयात का खेल"

जिंदगी की एक ही रीत है,
कभी हार तो कभी जीत है,
'क्या होगा' इस फ़िक्र मे आज गवा देते है हम,
'क्या हुआ था' ये भी सोच कर,
खुद को ही चोट पहुँचा देते है हम,
जिंदगी का हर पहलु हमे कुछ सिखाती है,
खुद के दिए घाओ पर मलहम भी,
खुद जिंदगी ही लगाती है,
जब-जब सुलझाने की कोशिश कि है मैने,
तब-तब शिकस्त के रूबरू हुए है हम,
ये तो समझ गए, सिख ही है जिंदगी के दिए हुए सारे गम,
कहते है एक दिन सबका वक़्त आता है,
ऐ-जिंदगी ऐसी क्या नाराजगी मुझसे,
जो मेरे खिलाफ़ चल रही है,
ना कल मेरी थी,ना अब मेरी हो रही है.....

जिंदगी की फरियाद

बहुत अरसे बाद, आज जिंदगी से मुलाकात हुई है,
ढलते शाम के साथ चाय पर,
जिंदगी से दो टुक बात हुई है,
मुस्कुरा कर जिंदगी आज मुझे ये समझा रही है,
मत कर अपनी मोहब्बत पर इतना ऐतबार, ये बता रही है,
उसकी मोहब्बत तेरी जिंदगी को बेरियो से जकड़ती है,
तु भागती है, गिरती है, अपने ही हयात से लड़ती है,
खुद को छुड़ाने की कई कोशिश भी करती है,
बाते सुन जिंदगी की खुद के बेबसी का एहसास हुआ,
दर्द जो महसुस नही होती थी,
अचानाक वो दर्द दिल के बहुत पास हुआ,
वक़्त गुजरता गया,
जिंदगी कई किस्से कह गयी,
एहसास हुआ उनकी मोहब्बत मे,
ये जिंदगी बहुत कुछ गलत सह गयी....

Maung Ibrahim

This is Maung Ibrahim I'm 18 years old, from Myanmar northern hamlet, Maung Daw Township Rakhine state (Arakan)

I'm one of the most persecuted and oppression, and also I was Myanmar golden student, but I can't learn more education due to civil war known as Rohingya minority in Myanmar so, we had fled neighboring country its Bangladesh because of racism or discrimination in own country or nation.

Life

We need to create a valuable life
The things are learning to empower life
With new stressful to solving
The refresh to be better to evolving,
Emotions of life movements,
have come to something improvements
What you have done with your exultant!
The matter of life, its consultant,
Do greatly your appreciated the life structure
Cuz your life not only your achiever
But also others life lesson by nature
Keep better feel with yourself
You have everything in your life
But without hard no gain on life
If you want to be ideal, you have to face more difficulties
I admit with you definitely reach your destination

Same Sentimental In My Life

Everything is sufficient to do with love
I want to show about my beloved motherland
There is so many things in my motherland
They are look like valuable and admirable,
Oh! My dear my motherland
I can't express how much I love you
I'm everything in my real life with you
Because I grew up on your surface,
Oh! Hello, see my second steps
About life partner how much enthusiastic in couple
Like the most beautiful in multiple
By grade and grade in principle,
O, my lovely sweetheart
You are my life partner
Still my last breath I spent with agitator
I take from you many kinds of things for my life creation.

Rashmi Yadav

She is Rashmi Yadav from Uttar Pradesh. She is currently pursuing her master's .she loves to write and express their emotions through her writings.she is currently working with 10 Anthologies.she believes"Being yourself whatever the circumstances".

Life Is A Secret Journey.....

Life is a secret journey,full of surprises and you never know what's next....
Life is a mashup cycle of different sensations
Life is full of tit for tat experiences
Life is a temptation dream,we expect something and we get something
So,If you wants to live your wealthy life then live on some principles
Because people don't have control on their emotions
Life stop's when pause comes then everything paused
So,enjoy every bit of your life as you never know what's next.......

शिकवे तो ज़िंदगी में हमेशा रहेगे पर जब गिलाओ में भी अच्छाइयां खोजोगे तब ज़िंदगी को और भी महकता देखोगे .

You can't watch a single episode
If you find it tedious similarly you
won't be able to live a monotonous
life that's why you found a lots of twists in life to make a intresting life.

Govind Narayan Joshi

A writer and Influencer

क्या फ़र्क पड़ता है यार

लोग क्या सोचते है
जीवन तो तुम्हारा है
सपने भी तुम्हारे है
ठोकर भी तुम्हे खानी है
मंजिल भी तुम्हारी है
रास्ते भी तुम्हारे है
दर्द भी तुम्हारा है
जीना भी तुम्हे है
चलना भी तुम्हे है
तो क्या फर्क पड़ता है
कौन क्या बोल रहा है

यादें भी होती है ज़िन्दगी में कुछ अजीब सी...
कुछ हमें जीने का हौसला देती है तो...
कुछ यादें हमें हंसने का मौका देती है....
तो कुछ हमे ज़िन्दगी की अनकही पहलू को रिझाने की...
जो भी हो पर यादें ही हमारा सबसे अच्छा साथी होता है...
यही है जो हमारी अंदर की अच्छाई और बुराई को बताती है...

Sukriti Chauhan

An enthusiastic Writer who wants to change the panorma of the society through her write-ups. She has a Passion for Writing Poetry, Articles and Blogs for her Website- (https://sukritichauhan1111.wordpress.com/) Besides ,She is also a Gold Medalist in Master's in English Literature. Whenever She is not writing, She can be found either Reading or Cooking.

Instagram handle- moondust_poetry

Sanctifying Wisdom

Life has a magical way of surprising us every time because When we expect something and it happens, suddenly we are so grateful that finally we have achieved that milestone but when something doesn't work out as per our expectations, we are shattered and disheartened and every second feels like a burden. This is human psychology and it's extremely normal to feel something like this, when we feel lost.

The only way to get back in track is to have faith in yourself and above all on your highest true self because the belief that everything is slowly working in your favour, perpetually shifts your negative energy into positive ardour which makes it easier to get things done but in order to attain it, one should always believe in making good deeds because every action of yours, be it good or bad has a count.

For Instance, if you see a person who needs help and you are capable enough to help him out but rather than helping him, if you tend to ignore him then there are possibilities that someday you will also go through a similar phase where you wouldn't be provided with any help from whomsoever. So, this is basically the ideology of "KARMA" also known as the cycle of Cause and Effect.

It's easy to inculpate the Situations, People or even the highest self for your failures but remember it's always your actions which determines your future and no one but your actions are responsible for that.

I ask the Lord When I feel Low,
Give Me Strength So that I can Grow.
I ask the Lord When I lose My Mind,
Give Me Reasons to be More Kind.
I ask the Lord When I Sense the Pain,
Give Me Endurance to Spring Again.
I ask the Lord When I Start to Regret,
Give Me Patience not to Fret.

Anjali Samundre

इस दुनिया से है अनजानी
दिल से है नादानी
आवाज़ से है रूहानी
भोले नाथ की दीवानी हैं अंजली

ज़िन्दगी

हँसने और हँसाने का नाम हैं ज़िन्दगी
सारे गमो को भुलाकर गले लगाने का नाम हैं ज़िन्दगी
रास्ते कठिन है इसके पर चलते जाने का नाम हैं ज़िन्दगी
गाने और गुनगुनाने का नाम हैं ज़िन्दगी
प्यार करने और प्यार निभाने का नाम हैं ज़िन्दगी
दिल टूटे आशिक़ हैं तो क्या बात हैं शायर बनकर एक दास्तां लिख
जाने का नाम हैं ज़िन्दगी
ढोकरे लगने पर भी एक नई शुरुआत का नाम हैं ज़िन्दगी।।

जीवन

सच भी जीवन झूठ भी जीवन
नई चाह और एक राह हैं जीवन।
धीरे-धीरे चलकर मंज़िल पर पहुंच ही जाएंगे
परेशानियां आयगी मोड़ में पर हम नही घबरायेंगे।
कभी हँसेंगे कभी रोएंगे भी पर अपने लक्ष्य पर पहुँच ही जाओगें, ये
जीवन एक चुनौती हैं इसे सफल करके दिखलाएंगे।।..

Raza Sahil

City- Amravati, Maharashtra
Profession- Central Government Employee (RAILWAY)
Passion- Poetry Writing

आप को जो ज़िंदगी पर एतबार है बहुत
फिर मसअला तो आपका दुश्वार है बहुत

मय्यत पर पहोच तो जाएंगे वक़्त पर
मसरूफ आज कल जो मेरे यार है बहुत

ऐ शाहज़ादी इश्क़ नहीं कर सकूंगा मै
के मुझ गरीब पे घर का भार है बहुत

मंज़िल पे ही नज़र रखे चलते रहो सदा
ये मत देखो कि इस राह में खार है बहुत

तुम एक ही शख्स से मिले हो जानेजा फकत
मुझ में छुपे हुए अभी किरदार है बहुत

तनहाइयों के खौफ से जो शख्स मर गया
अब मिल्कियत में उसके भी हक़दार है बहुत

आसां है जंग जीतना लेकिन मै क्या करूँ
मेरे कबीले में ही जो गद्दार हैं बहुत

एक दिन भंवर के बीच में डुबोएगा रज़ा
जिस शख्स पर भी आपको एतबार है बहुत

सब यार हमको जो बदनाम कर रहे हैं
हम है कि उनका ही अहतराम कर रहे हैं

हम इश्क़ ओ मुहब्बत को आम कर रहे हैं
मज़हब सिखाता है जो वहीं काम कर रहे हैं।

हम को खरीद ले साहिल अब किसी भी सूरत,
बाज़ारे इश्क़ में खुद को बेदाम कर रहे हैं,

वो आ बसा है हम में या हम उसी में कैद है
क्यों ज़िक्र उसका ही सुबहो शाम कर रहे हैं,

मालूम है हक़ीक़त हमको ये जानते भी है
क्यों आप बात को अब इबहाम कर रहे हैं

कुछ काम तो यक़ीनन मुझ से निकल के आया है
यूँ ही नहीं जनाबे साहिल सलाम कर रहे हैं

Sushant Kumar

sushant kumar is 29 year old working in quampetence buisness solutions. Also Co-director of event managment company Squad Talent Media.He is an amazing poet and he wants to be a known writer in future..

दास्तान-ए-जिंदगी

अब सह लेता हू हर ग़म मैं कायदे से मुस्करा के,
जिन्दगी जीना सीख गया हूं जिंदगी की डाँट खा के।
ना जाने कितनी बार बिखरा हूँ रिश्तों को निभा के,
अक्सर अपनों ने झकझोरा है गैर मुझे बता के।
अब तो गैर भी बदनाम करते हैं बुरा मुझे बता के,
तड़पता रहता है मेरा दिल बिना किसी खता के।
खैर धोखे का बवंडर भी गुजर जाता है धौंस अपना दिखा के,
हर बार कुछ ना कुछ अच्छा! जाता है मुझे सीखा के।
अब सह लेता हू हर ग़म मैं कायदे से मुस्करा के,
जिन्दगी जीना सीख गया हूं जिंदगी की डाँट खा के।
कोई कितना भी करे शिकवा या शिकायत मेरी जहां से,
मेरी नीयत मेरी आदत ना छुपी है उस खुदा से।
अब तो ज़माने की चलन को देख चुका हू आजमा के,
पुराने चेहरे भूल जाते हैं नए चेहरों को अपना के।
अब सह लेता हू हर ग़म मैं कायदे से मुस्करा के,
जिन्दगी जीना सीख गया हूं जिंदगी की डाँट खा के।

चलो आज खुद से खुद को लिखता हू मै

रोज परस्थितियों के आगे टिकता हू मैं,
अडिग रहता हू नहीं हिलता हू मैं।
टूट के कई बार बिखरता हू मैं,
फिर नए उल्लास के साथ संवरता हू मैं।
चलो आज खुद से खुद को लिखता हू मैं।

हूं साफ दिल का तो हर राह मे ठोकर खाता हू मैं,
गम मे रह कर भी खुशियों के गीत गाता हू मैं।
हर जरूरतमंद की उंगली पकड़ता हू मैं,
छल को खुद से हमेशा दूर रखता हू मैं।
कहने को होता है बहुत कुछ पर ना कह पाता हू मैं,
चलो आज खुद से खुद को लिखता हू मैं।

सब का भला कर के भी बुरा बन जाता हू मैं,
हर बार रिश्तों मे जोकर बन जाता हू मैं।
मजबूर होकर भी नहीं झुकता हू मैं,
चलो आज खुद से खुद को लिखता हू मैं।

Neha Singhal

Neha Singhal is an introvert until you initiate, one part of her wants to give up while the other keeps going. She kisses life poetically everyday and believes can of worms is not variants in the vicinity rather you yourself.

Imbue Yourself In Positivity

Life is just not about absorbing one human.
Go ahead and look upon the things you are grabing without any chase. Chasing will make your depression win. Don't overthink, it'll make you cry your soul out. No matter how much you pay your blood off if love is not meant to be it'll not. Take a break and start chasing yourself instead of chasing other being. Frame yourself with self-love and the specimens those who love you carrying blank reasons. Don't just end up being a living soul. Live through that demon inside you who actually appreciates the taste of life. Happyfy yourself with that one piece of cake instead of having a greed for the whole. Hold the positivity. Time never spells your emotion rather the piousness does. It is not mandatory to adore the one who ain't adoring you.
Get over the being as soon as possible if it's been a dog's age because even if you take a donkey's age that singleton is not going to adore you back. This is the bitter truth of life and the myth is which you live by of receiving a chase back. Sometimes absence of sound and emotion becomes bossy. If you still wish to chase take a lifespan of Guinea pig and adore yourself for a while. You'll veritably sense the peace and it might switch your emotions from one to another. Hence you'll start craving for those who crave for you.

Mousumi Sen

This Is Mousumi Sen Belonging From Jamshedpur. She Is A Student Curently In Her High School. She Possess A Hobby Of Writing And Dreams To Write A Book Of Her Own Soon. To Read More Of Her Writings Visit Her Instagram Handle.

Colours Of Life

Life Begins And End Illustrating A Band Of Divergent Shades,
Some Are Bright And Luminous Forever, While Some Eventually Fades.
Our Toddler Days Were Abandoned With Ticking Tones,
The Grounds Were The Virtue Along With Glee Got From Our Concerned One.
But As We Step Towards Being Matured As Well As Thoughtful Every Passing Day,
There Are Some Pearly And Darker Tinges Coming Along On Its Way.
In Our Teenage Days, We Came Across Love And Feelings,Depicting The Tint Of Pink And Red.
And Later Acknowledged That The Deeper You Dive, The Colours Become Variant,
Allowing The Exposure Of Pastels, Until You Complete Your Journey To The Death Bed.
After Witnessing The Ups And Downs,
The Way To The Life Midway Is Alike The Colour Purple And Brown,
Its When You Observe What's Happening All Around, Realising Its Time To Settle Down.
Some Day Its Black, Even Though Due To Peace And Harmony It Swaps To White And Blue,
Afterall Life Is Just Like A Rainbow Not A Single Hue.

For Fifteen Minutes Long I Kept Gazing At The Blue Sky That Day Just To Observe The Blirds Flying And How The Tress Were Fluttering Freely In The Open. That Day I Was Really Upset With Life And Had Just One Question In My Little Stormy Head," Does My Life Has A Value On The Superficial World? Am I Needed To Be A Part Of It?". It Was Quite Weird For A Teenager Who Was Barely On Her 9th Grade To Think That Way, Questioning About Her Existence But Who Cared To Notice The Fact That Sometimes Situations Make Us Think The Way We Aren't Meant To. Well After Have A Long Stary Observation The Only Thing Which Made Me Most Enthusiastic Was The Fact That Why Do These Clouds Have Such Interesting Shapes And Why Are They Moving In The Sky Constantly. Now Before Someone Portrays There Scientific And Geographical Knowledge Here Lemme State This, I Was A Kid Back Then. So I Decided To Look For An Answer And On The Voyage I Asked My Mom The Cause Of The Movment. She Exclaimed The Clouds Keeps On Moving Just To Shade The Sun Sometimes And Sometimes Moves Far Apart For The Sun To Show Its Ray. But Mostly It Doesnt Have Any Specific Reason But Still Its Important. And This Striked My Head And Answered To The Question Regarding My Existence Too,.

Sadhwika Suma

A writer by heart, “Sadhwika suma from Nizamabad Telangana”. Daughter of “Holapu Sudharshan and Vani”. Beginner with an Instagram page. 19 years old girl who is a daydreamer which dreams won’t let her sleep. She writes like she owns the beautiful things in the Universe. She writes her thoughts on very tiny things which happen in her daily routine. She lives happily with a dream to become an author someday. A strong believer in the love, hope, universe and it’s magic. She put her soul in her words. Many teenagers can feel the power of love and pain in her words. From normal quotes, writer at 17 to a become a poetess she proved herself as a writer. Her wings spread widely, and ink spills from the aorta of her heart. Writing makes her complete. She can pen with no boundaries… It took 19 years to realize her love towards the dam full of words in her heart, ready for the gates to be opened in the form of ink in her pen when finally destined herself to be a writer and a poet. And she had dream to inspire millions of people through her stories and poems. To fall in love with her writings visit Instagram:- @Sadhwika_writingsTo fall in love with her stories visit WordPress:-
www.sadhwikasuma.wordpress.com

Life Is A Mirror

Life is but a mirror,
Looking back at us.
Everything we do each day,
Should lead us to impress.
And sometimes when we need,
To see life differently.
We have that mirror to help us,
Change our view gently.
The eyes of everyone,
Also reflect back.
Mirrors come in different ways,
To show us what we lack.
But most importantly,
Don't forget to always look.
Be your best
And life will look after the rest.

What we see and what we do
Are reflections of what is true
Don't let your mirror reflect the things
That you do not want to come true.
Instead each day set your goals
Strive to complete, it is good for your soul.
Give life all you've got
Never look in the mirror and stop.

Titiksha Singhal

This poetry is written by Titiksha singhal. She loves to write poetries, stories and sometimes songs too. She is an engineer by profession but poetess by passion. You can connect with her at Instagram handle @titiksha_singhal

अब जी लो तुम

जिंदा तो हो तुम ,
क्या ज़िंदगी जी रहे हो ?
बेशक़ चल रहे हो ,
लेकिन क्या आगे बढ़ रहे हो ?
हर सुबह उठना और काम पर निकल जाना ,
न चाहते हुए भी, झूठी मुस्कुराहट मुस्कुराना ,
और फिर रोज़ की तरह, थक हार कर सो जाना ||
हर रोज़,
ना जाने कितने लोग,
कुछ ऐसी ही ज़िन्दगी जीते हैं |
ना हसते हैं, ना बोलते हैं ,
बस खोए खोए से रहते हैं |
आख़िर कुछ खुशियाँ तो ज़िंदगी में लाओ ,
रूखी सी ज़िंदगी को खुशनुमा बनाओ ,
हँसो, बोलो और बातें करों ,
अच्छी यादों को ताज़ा करो |
कुछ बचकानी ही सही,
पर वो बचपन वाली बातें,

फिर से करो|

माना ज़िन्दगी में दर्द बहुत हैं,
पर खुशियों की वजह ढूँढ़लो,
अपने काम को बोझ नहीं ,दोस्त समझ लो|
परिवार को जिम्मेदारी नहीं, सहारा समझ लो|
अकेले तो, ना जाने कितने लोग चलते हैं,
साथ देने वाले तो बहुत कम ही मिलते हैं|
तुम भी किसी का सहारा बनो,
दुसरो की खुशियों में ख़ुशी ढूंढ़ लो |
सात जन्मो का तो पता नहीं ,
पर इस ज़िंदगी को थोड़ा ही सही,
ज़ी लो तुम, बस अब जी लो तुम|

Priyanshi Mittal

Priyanshi , An enthusiastic writer who writes to pour her heart to the world to aspire it with her own experiences and feelings. Decorates her words with the depth of her heart and she believes that life is a journey with vivid twists and turns to be explored in every moment.

जिंदगी एक एहसास

खुशियों भरा ये सफ़र लौट कर ना आएगा
ना जाने कब कौन अनजान ये हसी चुरा ले जाएगा
तब बस अस्को की लड़ी होगी
ख़ामोशी हाथ थामे खड़ी होगी
ना कोई पास होगा
जाने क्या एहसास होगा
कुदरत का दरवाज़ा खटखटाना
तक़दीर को अपनी पास बैठाना
हज़ारों सवालों के जवाब की
लम्बी एक सूची बनाना
और नींद से जाग कर हौले से मुस्कुराना
दोनों हथेली जोड़ कर खुदा से गुहार लगाना
फिर कभी ऐसा स्वप्न हमें ना दिखाना

Manisha Sharma

Manisha Sharma from Pali Rajasthan is an Assistant Professor in Commerce and Management Studies by Profession and a Writer by Passion. She is pursuing her Phd in Accounting. She is co-author of various anthologies. She believes that "Either write something worth reading or do something worth writing." You never have to change anything you got up in the middle of the night to write.
Her Instagram handles are @ and @sachhi_kalam1709.
You can contact her on manishasharma1729@yahoo.com
Keep reading.

" Make The Real Jest Of Life "

This new year Let's pen our words more and more!
Lets bring out the best in ourselves.
I can always write for myself; but unlike other professions mine is not only for myself!
I've a responsibility to Motivate, Inspire, Counsel through my Writings!
Let my ink flow emotions; this year!
As the world turns 21, let's be more responsible and enjoy to the brim...
It's never too late to start again,
It's never too late to start at any point of time.
Whenever you are confident do start,
Because time doesn't matter but the will power does.
Whenever you feel you can do it,
Just start at that time.
Not just about starting anything,
But for apologising and ending also.
It's never too late to learn anything,
Age is just a number which keeps on increasing but the fact and life expectancy with dedicated doesn't decrease it keeps on increasing.

Whenever you feel you are done,
Do think once why you started and what was your goal?
Have you really accomplished what you had set?
Have you really achieved all what you really wanted in life?
If not don't stop,
Keep moving ahead.
Because life doesn't give second chance to everyone,
But it's fair enough that it's never too late to start and gain something.
So, be precise, prepared and dedicated,

And move on towards your goal as till life exists it's never too late for anything for anyone whether be it anything at any point of time!!

Some beautiful moments gone;
Some beautiful moments to come!
Many resolutions made;
But not all are said!
Some happy, some sad moments of life;
Make the real jest of life!

Pramesh Kumar

Pramesh Kumar, a writer who writes from his innermost.He is a budding and blooming personality in literature and in the literary world. He alway tries his best to put his head and heart on paper by his pen. His writing is very simple and understandable that people become friendly with his writing very easily. He is very clear and subtle in his writing and a person who pours down an ocean of thought in a flow of just a few words. He always gives his readers a direct way to his thoughts and life experience. His minute observation of worldly things and aspects gives a charm in his writing. After all he is a lover of nature and humanity. He is a happy go lucky person in his personal life. Whatever he writes he tries to give a personality to his poem which conveys his innermost to his reader.

He rightly says about his writing, "Every word of my writing is not only a combination of letters but my heartbeat which gives life to my literary arts".

जीवन: एक उतार चढ़ाव

कभी प्यार भरे बचपन में बीता
लिया जवानी के लहरों में गोता
कभी प्यार भरे दिन अक्सर बीते
कही कुछ मीठे लफ़्ज़ों को तरसे।
कभी माँ के बने हाथों से खाया
कभी ख़ुदका पकाया भी न अंग लगा
कभी पिता ने दिए कुछ गिनकर पैसे
कभी अपनाया कमाया भी न खर्च कर सका।
कुछ सुख के दिन सुहाने बीते
कुछ रातें बीती रुसवाई में
कुछ बीते लम्हें साथ साथ
कुछ बीते अक्सर तन्हाई में।
जीवन जीना जीने की कला
है कला कलम की करतब का कमाल
यहीं सुःख-दुःख है प्रेम क्रोध भी
है जीवन ऐसी उतार चढ़ाव।

Shariq Asghar AKA Samurai Sheikh

He Is 25 Year Old Man.He Resides In Faridabad(Delhi NCR).He Is An Engineer By Profession.Became Writer By Situation And Personal Life Experiences.
He Have Hunger For Knowledge Like A Craving Beast.

उड़ेगा उड़ेगा यह परिंदा पहली बार आसमान में ।
ज़रा इसे पंख तो फैलाने दो।
ग़म के बादल है तो क्या हुआ छंट जाएंगे एक बार खुशियों की बारिश में इसे नहाने तो दो।
ना रोको इसे किसी भी चीज़ से साथ दो इसका।ज़रा इसे खुल के आने तो दो।
पैसों और हवस की भूख नहीं। बरसों की भूख है इसे सिर्फ ज्ञान की । इसे जी भरकर खाने तो दो।
ना चाहता है यह परोसा हुआ थाली में। वक़्त को इसे अपनी कसौटी पर आजमाने तो दो।
उड़ेगा उड़ेगा यह परिंदा पहली बार आसमान में ।
ज़रा इसे पंख तो फैलाने दो।

Krishna Naresh Hire

Krishna living in Aurangabad Maharashtra, in bsc Ty , always want to try new things in my lufe

Life Lesson

Let Live life at one time
Make your own distinction
Make a new friends
Do whatever you want
Make a neww life
Things about it
Achieve something in life
Search a lifeline for lifetime
Which make you feel happier
Give him all happiness
An always feel every one happy
Live a life like a king
Lastly be happy an feel all happy
That life......
Love you and your family

Ashish Bharti

मेरा नाम आशीष भारती है फिलहाल पढ़ाई करता हूँ , मैं छिंदवाड़ा, मध्यप्रदेश का रहने वाला हूँ, मेरी उम्र मेरे सपनों से छोटी है। (22 साल)
"पढ़ लेना जो आज लिखता हूँ, शायर थोड़ा बदतमीज हूँ कुछ खास लिखता हूँ"

न सर का दर्द न आंखों में पानी आता था..
वो बचपन था जो भी आता था कुछ न कुछ दे जाता था...
न चिंता फिक्र न कोई भविष्य का डर था..
हँसना रोना शोरगुल और खिलौनों से भरा मेरा घर था...
सब खुश तो थे फिर मुझसे मेरे बचपन की डोर किसने तोड़ दी..
क्या पता जिंदगी ने छोड़ी मुझे या मैंने जिंदगी छोड़ दी।।
वो स्कूल वो यार और क्लास की टॉपर से प्यार..
वो झगड़े लड़ाई और सीनियर की मार...
कैसे कहु खुदको कैसे समझाऊ ये सफलता के पहले के काटे है..
कुछ अच्छा चाहिए आगे जिंदगी में तो खाने पड़ेंगे थोड़े चाटे है...
कुछ न बहेगा कुछ न मिलेगा सारे आंखों के आँशु तूने अब निचोड़ दी..
क्या पता जिंदगी ने छोड़ी मुझे या मैंने जिंदगी छोड़ दी।
क्या पता जिंदगी ने छोड़ी मुझे या मैंने जिंदगी छोड़ दी।।

तेरी यादों को में सहेजे हुए तू यादो को मेरी भूल गई..
मेरे हाथों को पकड़ कर चली थी जब पहली बार स्कूल गई...
यू तेरा मुझे बुलाके खाना खिलाना..
जूठी बोटल से अपनी पानी पिलाना...
जब टीचर की मार खाता था में, आंखे तू भी बंद कर लेती थी..
मेरे हाथों को फिर सहलाक़े गालिया तू भी उन्हें खूब देती थी...
अब भी तेरे सोने के बाद सोता हु मैं..
किसे बताऊ रात को अकेले में रोता हूँ मैं।
किसे बताऊ रात को अकेले में रोता हूँ मैं।।
जो यादे तुमने छोड़ी है वो यादे बहूत रुलाती है..
वो लड़की सपनो में आके बचपन मे वापस बुलाती है...
मुझे अब भी याद है जब हमारी आखिरी मुलाकात थी..
सोचा बोल दूं जो मेरे मन मे तेरे लिए आखिरी बात थी...
डर वो तेरा हमेशा के लिए छोड़ जाने का कभी गया ही नही..
सोचा छोड़ो जाने दो साथ है ये क्या कम है इसलिए मैंने उसे वो कभी कहा ही नही...
न जाने क्यों खुदको खुदमे थोड़ा थोड़ा खोता हूँ मैं..
किसे बताऊ रात को अकेले में रोता हूँ मैं..
किसे बताऊ रात को अकेले में रोता हूँ मैं।।

Jyoti Soni

She's a young teenager who loves to read and write. Fashion Designer by profession.

She's an introvert person for strangers and extremely extrovert person for the people she knows well.She learnt to love herself for who she is.She has been a part of various anthologies, including the India's book of record and Vajra book of record.

Adhuri Si Zindagi

Zindagi nikal jayegi,ye samjhane me ki mai galat nahi hoon!
Aur jab tak mujhe koi samajhna chahega,
tab tak shayad mai na rahoo!

Hum Tum Zindagi

Kuch dur tum chalo,kuch dur main chalungi!
Adhoori si iss zindagi ko,sath milkar hum pura karlenge!

Pragati Kumar Shrivastava

Pragati kumar shrivastava from suriwayan District Bhadohi kam working as business manager in wockhardt ltd

ज़िंदगी

हर किसी के जिन्दगी की अपनी अलग कहानी है।
हर शख्स खामोश है ना बदली ये जो ज़िन्दगानी है।

जुड़ा हुआ जो बचपन से हर रिश्ता था अपनेपन से।
जैसे जैसे बड़ा हुआ वो शमिल कैसे हुई बेईमानी है।

अपने गम से दुखी रहा ये जिम्मेदारी तो निभानी है।
लिखता हूँ जो शब्दों में कुछ बाते फ़िर भी छुपानी है।

हर शख्स क्यों नाखुश है जानकर सच फ़िर भी चुप है।
अपनी की हुई हर नाकामी किस्मत के सर मढ़ डाली है।

अपनी गल्तियों से सीखता नही करता क्यों मनमानी है।
अपना दर्द महसूस होता है देकर दर्द दूसरों को कहता है।

अपने किये हर कर्मो को जानकर नज़र अंदाज़ करता है।
बात गर फायदे की हो तो गलत बात को सच ठहरता है।

Deepika Kumari

देश की राजधानी दिल्ली में रहने वाली 'दीपिका कुमारी' जो कि पेशे से एक अध्यापिका है, अध्यापिका होने के कारण पढ़ना और पढ़ाना सदा ही इनके व्यवहार में रहा है। पढ़ते - पढ़ाते इन्होंने महसूस किया कि अपने विचारों को दूसरों तक पहुंचाने का एकमात्र साधन लेखन ही है और इसी कारण से एक लेखिका बनकर उभरी।

ज़िंदगी मजदूर की

होकर जीवन से मजबूर,
बना कर्म से वह मजदूर।
स्वाभिमान की रोटी लाने,
निकल गया वह घर से दूर।
भीख मांगने से अच्छा है
मेहनत की दो रोटी खाए,
सही मार्ग पर चलकर
क्यों ना पेट की प्यास बुझाई जाए।
पर समाज के इज्जतदार लोगों से
जब उसका पाला पड़ा,
तो जाना उसने कि इज्जत
शब्द का नहीं उन्होंने अर्थ पढ़ा।
मुझसे भी जाहिल है ये
पढ़ें लिखें प्रतिष्ठित लोग,
अपशब्दों से घायल कर मुझको
कहते खुद को शिक्षित लोग।
मॉल में जाकर खरीदारी कर
मोल भाव नहीं करते लोग,
लेकिन मेरे आकर समीप
मुझसे गरीब बन जाते लोग।
थोड़ा कम कर लो, सही लगा लो,
20 का 15 करते लोग,
मेरा ही पेट लगते हैं काटने
बिन समझे मजबूरी का रोग।
महंगे रेस्टोरेंट में जाकर
वेटर को टिप देते लोग,
उस टिप का हर्जाना भी
मुझसे ही भरते हैं लोग।

अरे भैया, ओ रिक्शेवाले !
हम रोज यहां से जाते हैं।
30 मत मांगो 20 ही ले लो
कहकर वो इतराते हैं।
अमीर तो क्या मध्यमवर्गभी मेरा दुश्मन बन जाता है,
उसकी बचत बैंक का पैसा भी मुझसे ही जाता है।

Prachi Sharma

She is Prachi Sharma. She lived in Ghaziabad district in U. P. She participated in more than 15 anthologies. She compile two anthologies WRITE TO FEEL NOT TO EXPLAIN and WRITER'S WORLD. Give your feedback on email (prachisharma51689@gmail.com). Instagram id (@sharma0162).

Life

Life means to live
Not to quit .

In life many problems will come
But that doesn't mean you give up.
You give up just bcz of problems.
That's wrong, try to understand this thing.

You are a fighter,
And you have to fight from every problem.
You win the fight but
You have fought with this all.

Don't give up, every problem will solve.
But you have fight
Fight for your dreams.
For yourself, for all.

Saumya Bhatia

Saumya Bhatia is a 21 year old Delhi girl. She is currently pursuing her post-graduation and soon to become a dietitian. She started writing as a hobby and now this hobby is slowly and gradually developing into passion. She aspires to be a writer and want to reach to people's heart through her writing.

Jashan-E-Zindagi

Kya khoobsurat zindagi banai,
Uss rabb ne,
Kya khoobsurat rang felaye,
Uss rabb ne,
Kya haseen zindagi banai,
Uss rabb ne,
Kya khoob rishte banaye,
Uss rabb ne,
Mana ki hai hum sab alag,
Apne apne mein,
Banaye gaye hai hum,
Rabb ke sapne mein,
Kya khoobsurat zindagi banai,
Uss rabb ne.

Choti Si Zindagi

Aankh khuli jab phli baar,
Janam meine lia tha,
Uss rabb ke vardan se,
Zindagi mein meine kadam rakha tha,
Kya khoob rang hai iss duniya mein,
Alag alag sabki pehchan hai,
Uske baad bhi zindagi sabki sath hai,
Ho Na Jan pehchan ek dusre se,
Magar zindagi toh sanjhi hai,
Ye khoobsurat rang hai yaha,
Kya baat hai,
Iss zindagi ke irado mein.

Jitesh Soni "Yash "

Jitesh soni " Yash “, is from raipur Chhattisgarh. He is a student as well a writer.
Penned by:Divyanshu Pandey"Bittu"
Instagram handle :@divyanshu8193
Writing is his hobby
and he is very passionate about it.

आखिर क्यों है तू ऐसी ऐ जिंदगी.
कभी हंसाती है तो कभी रुलाती है तू ऐ जिंदगी
कभी दिन के उजालों सा तो
कभी रातों की अंधेरों सी है तू ऐ जिंदगी
कभी गम के लिबास ओढ़े तो
कभी खुशियों की सौगात है तू ऐ जिंदगी
कभी शोर करते ख़ामोशी तो
कभी शांत आवाज है तू ऐ जिंदगी

कभी अपनों से शिकायत तो
कभी गैरों का प्यार है तू ऐ जिंदगी
आखिर क्यों है तू ऐसी ऐ जिंदगी
कभी रुठी सी हैरान है तो
कभी खुद से परेशान है तू ऐ जिंदगी
कभी बेतरतीब जवाब है तो
कभी अपने ही सवाल है तू ऐ जिंदगी
ना जाने क्या क्या है तू ऐ जिंदगी.

Nibraz Shameem

Nibraz is a final year bcom student from kerala. She is very much interested in writing as well as singing.. She is talented.. She believes in her own work and very hardworking person

Power Of My Life

And then i realised,
That to be more strong
More confident
I had to be less afraid
I had to be less depressed
I lost my fear
To gain my life
I lost my memories
To gain a new life
I lost my past
To gain my future

CROWN OF MY LIFE

I kneels down and sat,
My dreams became faded
And i knew i was done,
Done with everything
I was about to take my own life
But then started thinking..
About wearing belief as my crown
So that i can be a queen
A queen of courage and belief

Vidya Kala Agrawal

This is Vidya Kala Agrawal. I like to write in both language (Specially hindi). For more search me on google Vidyakala Agrawal quotes.

दास्ता ए ज़िन्दगी

थक गई हूँ ए ज़िन्दगी,
अब तो आराम दे
कितना चलाऐगा अब तू मुझे,
मौत का फरमान भी तो दे।
बहुत कुछ दिखाया और सिखाया है,
बतला कर अपनी सच्चाई,
बहुत ही हंसाया और रुलाया है।
तुम भी खराब नहीं,इंसान भी खराब नहीं,
समय ने सबको खराब बनाया है।
उंगली पकड़वाकर मौत का,
ज़िन्दगी से गले लगवाया है।
देख रही हूँ यही दुनिया की रीत है,
अमीर-गरीब में नहीं प्रीत है।
वो दिन भी जल्द आएगा
जब मतलब के लिए ही
इंसान-इंसान को ही मार गिरायेगा।
दिखा कर के झूठा प्यार,
जब खोखले रिश्ते बनाएगा,
तब भाग्य और समय,
दोनों ही उसे मार गिरायेगा।
गुरुर उसका फिर भी नहीं जाएगा,
थम जायेगी साँसे उसकी,
मौत का फरमान भी आएगा।
मुक्कमल होगी नींद उसकी,
आराम भी मिल जाएगा।

Varun Gupta

Varun Gupta is a working professional in the Aviation Group. He has done post graduation in the fields of Commerce. He is smart, witty and a charming person. His interest are playing badminton, football, cricket and he is fond of music, dance , yoga and writing. He has written many stories, poems and one liners. To know more about him, please follow him at instagram : iamvarungupta_088 and to learn about his writings, please follow him at https://www.yourquote.in/varun_gupta128

गुजरते लम्हें

जल तरंग सी बहती जिंदगी,
आज रुके पानी सा
गुजरते लम्हों को थामे हुए
आज रुके घड़ी के काटे सा।
कभी किसी भीड़ का हिस्सा
कभी किसी की बातों का किस्सा
कभी इक कहानी सा था जो
आज अल्फाज़ो के मोहताज़ सा।।
ज़हर सी हवा में घुला हुआ
भरी भरी गलियो में जो बढ़ा हुआ।
चीखती चिल्लाती वादियों में
खुद को फिर एक नज़र ढूंढता हुआ।।
आज एक कमरे में बंद सा।
मानो किसी कैद में जीता हुआ।
खुले सिर्फ़ विचारो और आशाओं की डोर में
कहीं बंधा तो कही बुना सा।।
एक नज़र खिड़की से झांकता हुआ।
है आदमी आज कुछ तंग और परेशान सा
रुकी जिंदगी को ताकता हुआ
गुजरते दिनों में खुद गुजरता हुआ ।।

Sumana Saha

A software engineer turned MBA-HR professional, she takes special interest in dancing, writing & social work. Currently associated with Cognizant HR Centre of Excellence – Compensation & Benefits, she has interned with multiple MNCs like Wipro before. She has written content for several startups, magazines, online pages, writing communities & blogs including her own blog Masqueraded Insurgence, and also published poems & stories with several publication houses. She is a trained Bharatnatyam dancer & has been part of renowned NGOs like United Nations' Volunteers India & CRY-Child Rights and YOU. In her free time, she likes exploring snippets, musing, and impactful microtales.

Twilight : The Cycle Of Life

Twilight, a transition it sure is,
From light to darkness and light again,
Bearing a close resemblance somehow
To the cycle of Life.
The morning of life is the dawn of a day
Full of purity, vision and harmony.
Dusk brings in darkness along with
Hope of new daylight yet again,
Celebrating the triumph of philanthropy
Over cynicism.
However, changes as inevitable
As sunshine,
Can be a friend or a foe,
A blessing or a curse.
A dawn or a dusk.

So, not knowing when the dawn will come
I open every door.

The Coveted Spring Of Light

The coveted spring,
Sprang up within,
Hoodlums of the nature..
Pathetic creature...
Their lecherous peep,
Still way too deep...lies
Failed courtship with their stomach...
Weeks, since the last crumb..
Of bread that slithered in ..
Lullabying hunger in broken slumber
Yet still awed by that cruel fruit..
That hangs above...
And shows him his place..
Mocking his debility
The hoodlums of nature..
Pathetic creature..
The castaway was here...
And they say spring feeds all...?

Divyanshu Pandey

Himself Divyanshu Pandey" Bittu" as he belong from Uttar Pradesh(Ballia district). His hobbies are reading, writing and talking to nice people.That's all about him.

Life is a Sinusoidal wave where Crest and Trough is necessary for growth.
If we believe in collaboration of Joy and Sorrow,then there is Curve.
With Two-outcomes either to leave that or Achieve that whatever I have planned.
I'm always trying to know the Secret of Life,
But I usually see that only this-Time is a key which will sudden -change you.
As a Member of Doctor,When any Cadaver came near me,
I appreciate to them that he is Free from his game.

A game where people are more sharper than Blunt -knife.
They always tried to cut your Fingers and Thigh.
Not with their Beautiful -Hands but by using Safety-Gloves.
Now, they are using their Brain to disturb your Mind.
If you Forget your Bad-moments and continuous in catching good moments,
Then Life will suddenly through you at Back,from where you came as a looser.
So keep remember while traveling to any Toughest-Path,
That I have to learnt golden-experience from this amazing Life.

Life is a Sinusoidal wave where Crest and Trough is necessary for growth.
If we believe in collaboration of Joy and Sorrow,then there is Curve.
With Two-outcomes either to leave that or Achieve that whatever I have planned.
I'm always trying to know the Secret of Life,
But I usually see that only this-Time is a key which will sudden -change you.
As a Member of Doctor,When any Cadaver came near me,
I appreciate to them that he is Free from his game.

A game where people are more sharper than Blunt -knife.
They always tried to cut your Fingers and Thigh.
Not with their Beautiful -Hands but by using Safety-Gloves.
Now, they are using their Brain to disturb your Mind.
If you Forget your Bad-moments and continuous in catching good moments,
Then Life will suddenly through you at Back,from where you came as a looser.
So keep remember while traveling to any Toughest-Path,
That I have to learnt golden-experience from this amazing Life.

Megha

She is a science student. She loves quotes, shayari and poems. Writing is my passion.
Instagram handle- @poems_lover7

जिंदगी की दौड़ कहीं गुम पड़ी है
कुछ डरावनी रातों में यूं गुजर रही है
सताये पलों को याद कर, निगाहें नम पड़ी है
सोचा नहीं था कभी जो सपनों में
ऐसी अंधेरी रातें आज मुलाकात कर रही है।।

बस ड़ायरी के पन्नों तक लिखने का जिगर पड़ा है
ये जमाना तो बस बदनाम करने को खड़ा है
ऐसी-ऐसी बातें बोलना लगा है ये जमाना
बिन सोचे- समझे बातें करना लगा है ये जमाना

क्या हुआ, क्या बीती है ये बातें में जानती हूँ
जिस्मों की भूख, खून के प्यासे लोगों को में पहचानती हूँ
मिटागें वो लोग अपनी भूख, छोड़ वहीं हालात में चलेंगे
दे गये तन पर दाग इतने और जिंदगी को नरक में धकेल गये ।।

Khushi

She is writer.

एक दिन यूंही बैठे - बैठे

एक दिन यूंही बैठे - बैठे कभी चलती कभी रुकती,
जाने क्या ही सोच रही थी ख्वाब अनोखे देख रही थी।
पूंछ रही थी सवाल अपने रब से क्या पूरे होंगे मेरे सपने कभी, क्या हो पाऊंगी मैं खुश भी कभी।
ये कैसी कशमकश है जिंदगी, खुश रहने में भी है मुश्किल कई।
हम बच्चे ही अच्छे थे बेवजह ही हंसते थे,
मन के भी सच्चे थे जब हम बच्चे थे।
खैर रब तो ना बोला मेरा ,
मुश्किलों ने जी टटोला मेरा,
बोला ये सब तो है किस्मत का खेला।
काफी देर बस यूंही सोच के,
फिर थक के खुद में ही सिमट के,
तकिए से लिपट के आंखे बंद करके ।
बोल पड़ी मैं जोर जोर से यूंही दिल में,
जो भी देखें हैं ख्वाब प्यारी ,
होंगे वो पूरे एक दिन, जरा रुक तो जा री।
कर यकीन भरोसा रख सपनो पे अपने,
रास्ते तो होते ही हैं मुश्किल हकीकत में,
डर मत चुन रास्ते तू अपने बेझिझक।
हर काम में अव्वल है तू खुद में,
तू है तेरे साथ तो फिर डर भी है कैसा,
जो जैसा मिले तू मिल उसमे वैसा।
जिंदगी गुलज़ार है ज़रा जी भर के जी तू,
आंखो से सपनो को बाहों में ले तू।
जिंदगी गुलजार है जरा जी भर के जी तू......

Ajay Kher

I am an Engineer by profession and writer by passion.

ज़िन्दगी

ज़िन्दगी भी क्या हैं,
समझो तो फर्ज हैं, ना समझो तो कर्ज हैं,
कभी लगती फूलों सी कोमल, कभी होती पत्थर सी कठोर,
कभी खुला नीला आसमान, कभी छाये घटाएं घनघोर,
कभी कराये इश्क खुद से, कभी दिलाये इश्क से दर्द हैं,
जिंदगी भी क्या हैं,
समझो तो फर्ज हैं, ना समझो तो कर्ज हैं,
कभी खून के रिश्तों पर, कभी रिश्तों के खून पर,
बहाती ये आँखों से दिल का दर्द हैं,
देती हैं बेशक हजारों गम मगर, बनती यही हमदर्द हैं,
समझो तो फर्ज हैं, ना समझो तो कर्ज हैं,
जिंदगी भी क्या हैं...

दास्तान ऐ जिंदगी

ज़िन्दगी की भी एक अजब सी कहानी हैं,
कभी करती इश्क़ हकीकत से,
तो कभी होती ये ख़्वाबों की दीवानी हैं,
कभी छलकायें आँसू खुशी के,
तो कभी बहाती आँखों से दर्द का पानी हैं,
ना रुकी हैं कभी, ना ही रुकेगी कभी,
ये तो दरिया का बहता पानी हैं,
ज़िन्दगी की भी एक अजब सी कहानी हैं...

Kalamkaar

This is Kalamkaar. He is from Uttrakhand bought up in Meerut(Up). His hobbies are reading and writing. His interest is in writing. He love writing. He is part of440+Anthologies as Co-Author. He won 490+ Certificate in Writing, He Start writing 29 February 2020. He is part of 7 anthology as Co Author going for record and He is omg record holder as Co - Author of Book Called Laposia. He is simple and people observer. His insta handle is kalamkaar51 and e-mail kalamkaar51@gmail.com. He believes in Karma.

सकारात्मक रहें

आये कितनी भी मुश्किल रहा मे।
ना डरे ना अपना उत्साह खोये।
जो करना हैं सफल होने मे।
अपने लक्ष्य तक पहुंचने के लिए प्रयास करें।
ना हो हताश अपने अंदर ऊर्जा को करें उत्पन्न।
ना हो असफल और कार्य सारे हो सम्पन।
रखे अपने अंदर हौसला, करते जाये कार्य।
रखे भरोसा अपने अंदर, होगा तुम्हारा जो लिया ख़ुद के लिए फैसला।
मिलेगी सफलता एक ना एक दिन तुमको।
और होंगे सारे काम पूरे जो छोड़े अधूरे।
किया नहीं भरोसा जिसने और करा तुम्हारे हौसले को नीचे।
बनो इतने सफल जो लोग तुम्हारी तरफ आ जाये खींचे।
उठाना ना कदम वो जिससे तुम्हें हो नुक्सान।
करना कड़ी मेहनत क्योकि होता नहीं सफलता पाने का रास्ता आसान।
आ जाये कितने उतार चढ़ाव मत करना अपने पे सवाल।
क्योकि वो तुम सबसे बढ़िया और हो तुम बाकमाल।
हालातो से हारकर मत सोचना नकारात्मक
करना भरोसा खुदपे और अपनी काबिलयत पर रहना हमेशा सकारात्मक।

Rutvik Borade

Hi I am software engineer, I starting write poem from past 2 year and still enjoying to learn more .I have published one book under my name.

Tu apni zindagi ka chalak tu khud he hein
Phir tu dusre ki marzi se kyu chalta hein??
-Zindagi ko zindagi ki tarah Jeena sikh ....

Tere ankho ke Ansoo tu khud hein nikalta hein
Phir tu dusre ke hatho se usse kyu mitata hein ???
- Zindagi ko zindagi ki tarah Jeena sikh ....

Tere di se nikli huyi awaaj tu khud sun sakata hein
Phir tu apne dil ki awwaj dusro ko kyu sunaat hein???
Zindagi ko zindagi ki tarah Jeena sikh ....

Teri nazar ke aage sahi aur galat ko khud padh sakta hein
Phir tu dusre ki nazar kyu padtha hein???
-Zindagi ko zindagi ki tarah Jeena sikh ....

Teri har mushkil bole bina khuda dekh sakta hein
Phir tu ankho mein ansoo lake unhe kyu dikhata hein???
Isliye kehta hoon zindagi ko zindagi ki tarah Jeena sikh

Vijeyata Joshi

आप विजेयता जोशी। कल्याण शहर के वाड़ेघर गांव से रेहेने वाली हूं। ये लेखक नहीं है ना इनके परिवार में कोई लेखक है, पर वे अपनी मां के लिए एक बुक लिखना चाहती हैं। उसी की कोशिश ये थोड़ा बहुत लिखने की कोशिश करती है। पेशे से ये एक pvt कंपनी में नौकरी करती हैं। इन्हें नई चीजें सीखना, लिखना, रंगोली, चित्रकला, हस्तकला, गुमना - फिराना , शॉपिंग करना पसंद है। इसे पहले और दो पुस्तकों में इनकी रचनाएं आई है

१. Lessons to remember

२. गोपियाँ - किशन जी दीवानी

ज़िंदगी क्या है,..........

ये घर से निकलने को बाद पता चलता है
स्कूल-कॉलेज खत्म होने के बाद पता चलता है
ट्रेन और बस के धक्के खाने के बाद पता चलता है
खुद कमाने लगने के बाद पता चलता है
पहेली तनख्वाह हात में आने बाद पता चलता है
विश्वास टूटने पर पता चलता है
ख़ून के रिश्ते ही साथ ना दे तो पता चलता है
कमाए हुए पैसे ख़त्म हो जाए तो पता चलता है
जीवन में आने वाले सुख दुख से पता चलता है।

ज़िंदगी से हार चुकी हूं, फिर भी जीतना चाहती हूं
ज़िंदगी से बार बार ठोकरें लगने बाद भी उठना चाहती हूं

ज़िंदगी में कभी कभी लाख कोशिश के
बाद भी कुछ चीजें हासिल नहीं होती,
दुख ये नहीं हमने जो चाहा वह नहीं मिला,
दुख ये है हम पूरी ज़िंदगी कोशिश ही
ग़लत जगह कर रहे हैं।

कहते हैं,
जिंदगी में ठोकर लगने से इंसान मजबूत हो जाता है,
पर ठोकरे इतनी भी ना लगे कि इंसान मजबूर हो जाए

Rachiyata

Her name describe herself Rachiyata, poet writer
She loves writing & dancing. she belives life is too short to be Sad so live everymoment to the fullest. She wanted to be remembered with a Smile in someone face!!

Farq Nai Padta!

Toot gaye mujhe
Toot ke chahne wale
Ab ye Dil kisi k liye
Dhadkata hi nai
Aisa suna hai
Logo ko kehte huye
Meri zindagi mein
Koi rahe na rahe
Mujhe farq padta hi nai
Magrur si apni zindagi mein, Mashruf hu
Koi pasand kare na kare
Mujhe Farq padta hi nai
Toot gaye mujhe toot k chahne wale
Ab Ye dil kisi k liye Dhadkta hi nai

Nasreena

Nasreena a reserch scholar from kashmir valley,U.G.C NET qualified in English literature, co-author of anthologies like life, miracles, ek nari sab pe bari etc,

"My Beloved As Moon"

When the moon and stars shine high
In the dark vast sky.
Only i see is
The light of your shine and sparks.
The hidden beauty of stars and moon
Can't be seen by me alone.
My mind and heart is full of you
And the light of your shine.
But when i see your presence
Between the dark bunch of hairs.
I can feel it like
The stars in the dark night.
So, when i found n see you
I needn't see the moon.
the anchor will be cut down
And my boat will sale again.
For i know how it feel n looks like
As Beautiful and charmfull you are.

Shubham Borade

Hey, this is Shubham Borade.
He writes love. He writes tranquil and deep feelings from which I've actually gone through. I'm still a unemployed fellow at my age of 24 running.
For me basically writing is just scribbling your feelings on notepad.
You can see my more write-up's on ig at @fadedone__ .

Kabhi chup sa hun,
Kabhi gum sa gaya hun apne manjil se,
Rastoon mai badh si gayi hai ab daarare,
Cahata hun koi mera haat tham le.

Mushkilon se na koi bach saka hai, aur na aisa koi jisne aj thokare na khai hai,
Pairoon mai bedhiyaa bandhi hai aur jindagi ban chuki ek gehari khaii hai.
Aasmaan mai udana cahate hai sab par umeedon ko aj pankh nahi hai,
Raahonn ki duriyaa bhapne chale aj toh ginti mai utne aank nai hai.

Bhool jana aasan lagne laga hai par sapne aj bhi sirf naakamayabiyon ke ate hai.
Agli subha jab aankhn khule toh najare firse wahi hai.
Bachpan kudh ko ye samjha kar gava diya ke bade hokar jindagi aasan honi hai,
Par kisi ne ye kyun nahi bataya ke sirf umar badh rahi hai par halat aj bhi wahi hai.

Na jane kab tak inn kathinaiyon ko paar karna hai aj,
Kya humare sar par bhi kabhi sajega khushi ka taj.
Ha maana agar mehanaat karo toh sab mumkin hai,
Par waqt ke haat kisi ke bas mai nahi, Kaise kudh ko nayi ummeed de?

She's humane. That's all that matters.

The joys that seem irrelevant
The loves that felt too faked
The chances let go of
Pour me a glass of your finest wine
They said I'd dined with the devil
Was he the one behind the mask?
My lifetime was worthwhile
Because I loved and liked wholeheartedly
My last breath is worthwhile I guess
Because I have no regrets.

Vivacious I should be
Making memories and memories making me
Your flaws I chose to ignore
Because I loved you with your very soul
Let's make more memories shall we?
Or make love under the moonlit skies
My life I want to be full
But only full with you.

Safeer Bhola

Located in Pune, India, I am a freelance digital content strategist cum poet who is on a mission to help to influence people through his words.

Started as a hobby in 2014, poetry has helped me in creating content that speaks to micro audience groups. As a poet, I have had the opportunity to headline as aguest performer at Pune International Literary Festival(2017) and to compile a poetry anthology "Speak" which was an Amazon Hot New Release and Bestseller. I have also been awarded a National Youth Award for Excellence in Creative Expression from the Aga Khan Youth and Sports Board for India.

While I have always used the power of words to entice audiences on social and personal issues, I have recently also entered the world of product marketing to bring values to companies in every domain.

Thoda Khulke Ji Le!

Kyu bhaag raha he pyaare
Kis cheez ka dar he tujhe?
Ek hi zindagi hai
Thoda khulke ji le!

Fir kal tu so jayega
Aaj jaagkar sapne dekh le!
Fir kal tu kho jayega
Aaj jaagkar nai raahe tu khojle
Ek hi zindagi hai
Thoda khulke ji le!

Fir kal tujhe yaad kar koi royega
Tu aaj usi ki zindagi banane ko chalde
Fir kal tujhe bhulane tere likhe khat ko koi jalayega
Tu aaj unme likhe shabdo ke jazbat ko amar karne ko chalde
Ek hi zindagi hai
Thoda khulke ji le!
Fir kal tu yaha hoga nahi
Par ye duniya tere kiye kaam ko yaad karegi
Fir kal tu yaha hoga nahi
Par ye duniya tere diye pyaar ke paigam ko padhegi
Agar sachme ye makaam pana chahta he tu
To ek hi zandagi hai
Thoda khulke ji le!

(2)

“Tufano ko takkar dene waale
Aaj lehro se dar ke bhaag rahe he
Manzil ko diya lekar dhundne waale
Aaj khuli roshni me raasta kho baithe he
Zindagi ko jo mehfil ki tarah saja kar rakhte the
Aaj wo use matam ka mahol banaa baithe he..”

Saurabh Tripathi

This is Saurabh Tripathi born in Chitrakoot UP. a person who had just finished his Post graduation. But all of the above and more than anything first i am a Writer with Poetic accent. And yes one page is not enough for introducing me but because i am Poet too so this is my responsibility to introduce in few words.For reading more of me or you can say my writings so go to my instragram page @theworldforwrite . You can also contact me on my your quote id - saurabh_tripathi

instragram - @theworldforwrite.
Mail id - theworldforwrite@gmail.com
Twitter - @WorldForWrite , @humanitysaurabh

बस हवा ही तो है।

कभी हवाओं से दोस्ती की है
कितनी सच्ची हैं ना
हर वक्त वही आवाज वही रंग वही रूप वही महक,
हर पल को छू कर निकल जाती पर हमेशा साथ होती।
ख़ामोश मगर तुमसे हमेशा तुम्हारी ही बातें करती,
हमारी हर गुनगुनाहट पर गुनगुनाती,
हर उदासी को खुशी में बदल जाती।
कभी बादलों को छूकर तुम्हे भिगो देती,
तो कभी सूरज सी गर्म होती,
कभी चांद की शीतलता में शरारत है करती।
हर महक में समाती , हर महक को ले जाती।
सब के लिए हमेशा बराबर सी,कमाल है ना।
कमाल की बात तो ये है ना आपके आखिरी वक्त में भी ,
आपके बाद जाती, तभी तो आखिरी सांस कहलाती।।
हवा ही है जो हरदम साथ निभाती,
पहली सांस से तुम में आके बस जाती,
और आखिरी सांस तक जाती।
सच्ची दोस्त कहलाती।।
पर क्या कहें बस हवा ही तो है, है ना।

Sarabjot Purba

सरबजोत पुरबा कोटकपूरा, पंजाब में रहते है। जब वो बारवीं कक्षा में थे तब उन्होंने पहली बार एक कविता लिखी। इसके बाद ई.टी.टी. की पढ़ाई करते समय उन्होंने कविताओं के साथ-साथ निबंध और कहानी भी लिखनी शुरू की। उन्होंने ने अपने मन के विचारो को एक किताब का रूप दिया है। जिसका नाम 'कुछ विचार' है। उन्होंने ई.टी.टी. कालेज का समय भी लिखा है। जिसमें उन सभी यादो को लिखा है जो उन्होंने ई.टी.टी. में बनाई थी। उन्होंने हर विषय पर कुछ न कुछ लिखा है। अक्सर वो समाज के मुद्दों पर लिखते है। वे ज्यादातर पंजाबी भाषा का प्रयोग करते है।

आजाद परिन्दा

मैं हुँ तो आजाद परिन्दा,
लेकिन उड़ने से मैं डरती हुँ।
कोई उड़ने भी तो नहीं देता,
कोशिश अकसर करती हुँ।
हंसती हुँ मैं सबके आगे,
लेकिन छुप कर आहे भरती हुँ।
सपने में ऊँचा उड़ती हुँ,
लेकिन गिर कर अंत में मरती हुँ।
मैं हुँ तो जलता दीया,
सबको रूशनाना मेरी औकात नहीं।
मैं रोशन होना चाहती हुँ,
लेकिन जिन्दगी में प्रभात नहीं।
जब बिन रोए मैं सोई हुँ,
मुझे याद भी ऐसी रात नहीं।
सब समझा कर मुझे जाते है,
कोई समझता मेरी बात नहीं।
मैं हुं तो एक नारी,
मरदो से आगे जाना है।
एक नारी क्या कर सकती है,
सबको यह बताना है।
हमारा हक हमें चाहिए,
हक हमें भी अपना पाना है।
औरत की क्या अहमियत है,
सबके आगे लाना है।

Flairs and Glairs, a platform by a student for the students. We are esteemed youth struggling to carve out our path for our future and we follow a basic mindset Since everyone is not born with all-round skills. Joining hands with people who are born to execute it with perfection is the best way to evolve. Self-Evolution is the need of the hour but, evolving as a community is what we strive for. The initiative as kickstarted by, Founder- Mr. Shubham Shah with the motive to utilize the skillset and talent of writing has now a team of 10+ people who are actively participating into newer forms of learning and discovering talents among youngsters. We Provide platform and services like Publishing opportunities, Open mics, Workshops, Hands-on training. Operating with Brand Name of Flairs and Glairs (Publication House), we offer the chance of elevating a passionate writer to an esteemed author With Brand name Teekhe Zasbaaat. We bring to you an opportunity to get accustomed with the Public Speaking and Presenting of Thoughts along with regular challenges to brush up your inking spirit. The newest initiative to extend our services we introduced in a new writing Platform- The Glittering Fables and Ink Over Tears.

We Choose to Fly Like A Falcon than to be

a Leg Pulling Crab.

To Know More: Infoline – 7781900870
Mail Us At-
flairsandglairs@gmail.com / info@flairsandglairs.in
Or Visit is at
www.flairsandglairs.com / www.flairsandglairs.in
Social Handles- @flairsandglairs @teekhezasbaaat

www.ingramcontent.com/pod-product-compliance
Ingram Content Group UK Ltd.
Pitfield, Milton Keynes, MK11 3LW, UK
UKHW022004190726
13853UKWH00004B/1729